BANTAM
OF THE OPERA

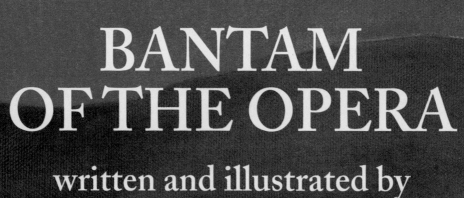

BANTAM
OF THE OPERA

written and illustrated by
MARY JANE AUCH

Holiday House/New York

For Roger and Donna Jestel,
good friends who taught me everything I know about chickens.

Library of Congress Cataloging-in-Publication Data
Auch, Mary Jane.
Bantam of the opera / written and illustrated by Mary Jane Auch.
p.   cm.
Summary: Luigi the rooster wins fame and fortune when the star of
the Cosmopolitan Opera Company and his understudy both come down
with chicken pox on the same night.
ISBN 0-8234-1312-8
[1. Singers—Fiction.   2. Opera—Fiction.   3. Rooster—Fiction.
4. Humorous stories.]   I. Title.
PZ7.A898Ban   1997   96-40169   CIP   AC
[E]—dc21

Luigi was hatched a bantam rooster, but he had the soul of a musician. When the other young roosters began testing their voices, they all crowed, "Cock-a-doodle-doo."

Not Luigi. "COCK-ala-DOOdle-y-DIDdle-y-DOO," he sang to the rising sun. "COCK-ala-KOOK-ala-KICK-ala-*CHOO*!"

"Knock it off," said the head rooster. "Nobody likes a show-off."

"But I get bored crowing the same old thing," said Luigi.

"Read my beak!" said the head rooster. "It's 'Cock-a-doodle-doo.' Got that?"

Luigi tried humming, so he wouldn't attract attention, but that wasn't as much fun as really letting loose. He tried sticking his head in a haystack to muffle the sound, but he almost smothered himself. Finally, Luigi wandered farther afield each day, so he could sing without being heard.

One afternoon on the farmer's porch, Luigi heard opera music coming from the radio inside. "I knew there was more to life than 'Cock-a-doodle-doo!'" he cried.

After that, Luigi sang along with the radio operas every day. His favorite aria was "La donna è mobile" from *Rigoletto*.

"Cock-a-la-DOOdle-lay," he crowed. He had learned it by heart.

Then one day, the radio announcer said, "The Cosmopolitan Opera Company is in our city for three performances of *Rigoletto*."

Luigi heard the farmer's wife say, "Wilbur, I do believe I'd likc to see that. What say we go tonight?"

A chance to see *Rigoletto*? Luigi almost fainted from excitement. That evening he slipped into the back of the farmer's truck and went to the city.

The opera was even more magnificent than Luigi had imagined. He could barely keep from bursting into song, especially during the solos by the famous tenor, Enrico Baldini. That night, the little bantam made an important decision. When the farmer drove home, Luigi was not in the back of his truck.

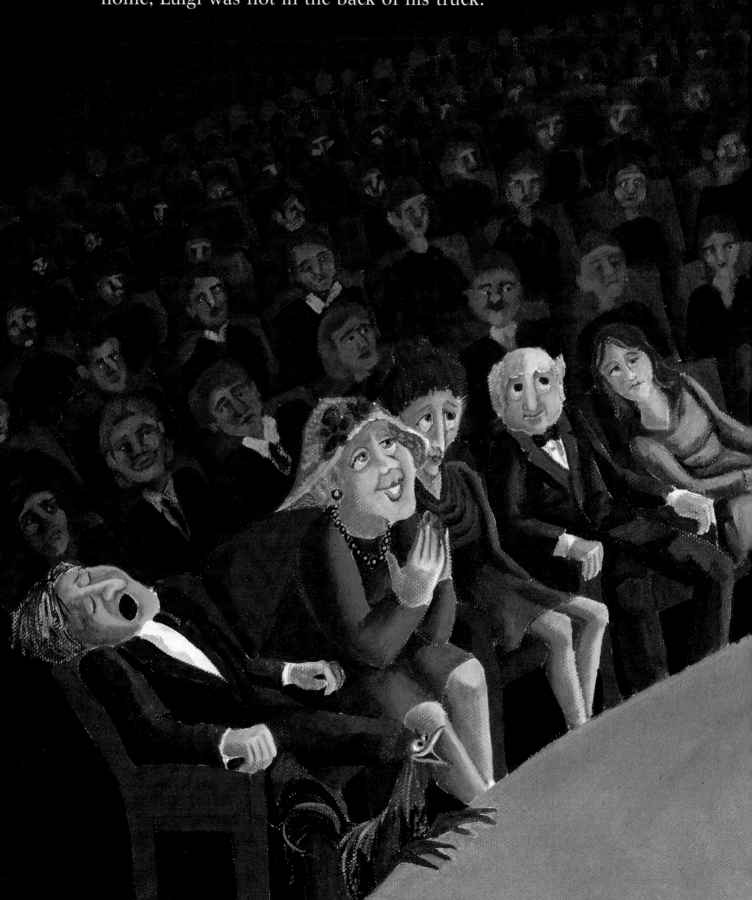

The next day, Luigi perched in the balcony of the darkened theater, watching the rehearsal. But when the orchestra played some familiar notes, he couldn't help himself. "Cock-a-la-DOOdle-lay. Cock-a-la-DOOdle-low," Luigi crowed, flying down to the stage. Baldini stopped singing, but Luigi kept going, his bright feathers gleaming in the spotlight.

"Get that chicken out of here!" Baldini screeched.

"The rooster has a lovely voice," said Carlotta Tetrazzini, the soprano. "And perfect pitch—so rare in a tenor."

"Perfect pitch?" Baldini lunged for Luigi, scooping him up by the tail. "I'll perfect pitch this poultry right out of the theater!"

As Baldini wound up, Carlotta stopped him. "Don't be a bully, Baldy. A singing rooster is the perfect opera mascot."

"All right," Baldini grumbled. "But the next time I hear one of my tenor arias coming from your chicken lips, I'll make noodle soup of you!"

That night, poor Luigi watched the second performance of *Rigoletto*, promising himself not to utter a note. But when Baldini started singing "La donna è mobile," Luigi lost all control. People looked to see where the second tenor voice was coming from. Finally the spotlight found Luigi, crowing his heart out from the great crystal chandelier.

Luigi flew off to another hiding place, but Baldini had seen him. After the performance, Baldini searched for Luigi with murder in his heart and a skillet in his hand. "Come out, you cowardly, conniving, copy-cat cockerel! I'll carve you into cacciatore!"

Luigi hightailed it through the backstage shadows and ducked into an open dressing room just in time to avoid being caught. "Exactly what I need," he said, looking at all the costumes.

He had found the perfect disguise.

That night Luigi watched from high above the stage. As much as he longed to sing, he didn't open his beak. Down below, the singers were warming up when suddenly Baldini started to scratch. Soon he was dancing around the stage, scratching with both hands. "I itch all over," he wailed. "It's driving me crazy."

The director squinted closely at Baldini's face. "You're covered with red spots! You can't perform like that. Where's Romeo Manicotti, your understudy?"

Manicotti dashed onto the stage. "Here I am, sir, all dressed, all warmed up. Ready to become a star!" Baldini went off into the wings to scratch and sulk.

"Not a minute too soon," said the director. "Places everyone."

Suddenly, Manicotti started to scratch and scratch ... and SCRATCH!

"You have the spots, too!" said Carlotta. "The curtain is going up any minute. No one else knows the tenor part!"

Luigi took a deep breath and flew to center stage. "Tah DAH!"
The soprano recognized him in spite of his disguise.
"I warned you," roared Baldini, rushing back on stage.

"Leave him alone," said Carlotta. "He's our only hope."
"But he doesn't sing the words," sputtered Baldini.
"Lighten up," said Carlotta. "Who understands the words?"
"He's terribly short," whined Manicotti.
"Big deal," said Carlotta. "So he sits on my shoulder."

Luigi's little bantam heart almost burst from joy as the great velvet curtain began to rise. But he hadn't counted on the reaction from the audience.

"Get a load of the beak on that tenor!"

"That's no tenor—it's just a chicken."

"Well, he's nothing to crow about!"

"Get off the stage, you dumb cluck!"

Luigi kept singing, in spite of his broken heart.

Soon his sweet voice soared above the jeers, and when he sang "Cock-a-la-DOOdle-lay," a hush fell over the audience. At the end, they gave him a standing ovation with six encores—three more than Baldini had ever received.

Luigi went on to become the most popular tenor of the Cosmopolitan Opera Company. To this day, Baldini and Manicotti blame Luigi for giving them the itchy red spots that kept them from singing that fateful night.

But everybody knows you can't catch the chicken pox from a real chicken …

or can you?

THREE TENORS